CAPTAIN NO BEARD AND THE Aurora Borealis

A CAPTAIN NO BEARD STORY VOLUME 7

Written by Carole P. Roman

To Zachary–

Welcome to our wacky crew!
We've been waiting for you.

Captain No Beard blew on his fingers to warm them up.

"It sure is cold, Captain." Hallie closed her coat to her chin.

Snowflakes floated down, and she heard Mongo the monkey call out,
"Iceberg, off the ship's bow!"

All of the crew rushed to the side of the ship, gasping when they saw the giant ice mountain.

"Well, blow me down!" Linus the lion roared.

"Shiver me timbers!" Captain No Beard shouted.

Cayla reached out, trying to touch it,
but Captain No Beard pulled her back to safety.

Polly the parrot flew overhead with a hammer in her beak and chipped away at the side. "I'll bring you some of the ice!" she called out to Cayla.

The sky was pitch black. Mongo handed Captain No Beard his telescope and asked, "Where are we going, Captain? My timbers are shivering pretty badly! It's late, and I'm cold. Brrrrr." His teeth clicked as they chattered.

Hallie wrapped a scarf around his neck to warm him up.

Captain No Beard peered through the telescope.
"Up there is the North Star—we are heading due north."

"You mean Polaris?" Hallie pointed to the bright light in the sky.

"Yes, that's its other name," Captain No Beard said. "I read in a book that
Polaris hardly moves, while all the stars around it change positions.
We use it to find our way north."

"Due north!" Fribbet hopped around. "It's late; we should head home.

Oh no,

I don't like this. Why are we heading north?"

"We are on a mission," Captain No Beard confided.

"A mission?" Linus growled. "What kind of mission?"

"We're pirates, right?" the captain asked him.

"Aye, pirates, we are," Hallie agreed. Cayla shook her head and tasted the chunk of ice. She wailed loudly. Her tongue was stuck to the surface.

"Cayla!" Hallie gently removed her from the icicle. "You can look at it, but don't taste it!" Not to be distracted, she asked again, "What are we going to do?"

"We are going to take something away from its home in the north and bring it to our place," Captain No Beard stated.

The crew reared back with shock.

"Take it away! Bring it home! What?" Linus shouted.

"I don't know about this. Did you ask for permission?" Polly fluttered around them.

The captain shook his head. In a small voice, he said, "No."

Mongo scratched his head.
"Taking something without permission is wrong."

"Captain, that's stealing," Hallie said in a shocked whisper.

"But we are pirates!" Captain No Beard pushed out his lip stubbornly. The crew turned their backs while Captain No Beard watched the horizon.

The crew gathered together, not liking this idea.

"I won't do it!" Linus stated.

"It's wrong. Someone has to tell him," Mongo added.

"I'm not that kind of pirate. I mean, I love treasure and all, but only if it doesn't belong to someone else," Hallie said reasonably.

"You can't take things without permission!" Fribbet yelled. "Someone has to tell the captain! We could get in trouble. I don't want to get in trouble." He hopped around the deck.

All the crew agreed: "Arrrgh, arrrgh, arrrgh!"

Captain No Beard paced the deck.

"Don't tell me I have to do this all by myself.

Being a captain is hard work," he muttered unhappily.

Hallie approached him.
"What did you want to take home, Captain?"
she asked gently.

"Look!" He pointed to the sky. It was getting brighter.
Hallie stopped and stared.

"Oh my!" she whispered.

All above them the sky was streaked with beautiful colors.

Greens mixed with pink, purple fading to blue.

It was as if someone was painting the sky.

"What is it?" Polly asked.

"The aurora borealis," Captain No Beard said. "I want to take it home."

"We can't do that!" Hallie told him.

"Why? It's not fair that it's only here. I want to look at it all the time!" he complained.

"First of all, it's not right to steal. I won't be a part of it, Captain," Polly said as she flew over his head.

Captain No Beard hung his head. "I wasn't going to steal it. I only wanted to borrow it for a little while."

"Second of all, you can't take the aurora borealis—it's part of the sky.
It only happens here because of the location and the weather.
It won't work at home," Hallie informed him.

Captain No Beard said very sadly,
"I love the aurora borealis. I want to look at it all the time.
What are we going to do?"

"I think I may have a solution," Hallie said with a smile. "Come on, Alexander! Oops, I mean Captain No Beard."

Captain No Beard followed her below deck.

* * *

The sun rose, and the children found themselves back in Alexander's bedroom, with brightly colored paper stuck on the walls all around them. Alexander smiled as he looked at his own personal aurora borealis.

"Great idea, Hallie!"

"Aye!" She winked.
"You can go anywhere or do most anything you choose with some paper and crayons!"

"And your imagination!" Little Cayla added.